E
 Wasson, Valentina Pavlovna, 1901-1
 The chosen baby.

 Rev. ed.,
 p. ;

THE CHOSEN BABY

THE CHOSEN BABY

by Valentina P. Wasson

Illustrated by Glo Coalson

J. B. Lippincott Company / Philadelphia and New York

U.S. Library of Congress Cataloging in Publication Data
Wasson, Valentina Pavlovna, 1901-1959.
The chosen baby.
SUMMARY: Because they want to share their home with
children, a couple adopt a boy and later a girl.
[1. Adoption—Fiction] I. Coalson, Glo. II. Title.
PZ7.W26Ch9   [E]   76-41391   ISBN-0-397-31738-7

FOREWORD

The Chosen Baby has served as a handbook for adoptive parents and their adopted children through the years since its first edition in 1939. Its magical effect continues mainly because it gets across to the child the sheer joy, the rapture, his adoptive parents experienced upon his coming into their lives and their satisfaction in having him as their very own.

Now brought to life in this revised edition by illustrations more realistically depicting our times, the story is as charming and delightful as when first told to the author's own son so many years ago. Relieved of the concept of "chosen" beyond its winsome title, the book gives an accurate account of what happens when a baby is adopted. It is meant for very young children and is best used as a background against which adoptive parents may spell out the specifics relating to their own child's adoption. It is recommended as a most agreeable way to begin the continuing process of telling a child about adoption.

LOYCE W. BYNUM
Associate Executive Director
Spence-Chapin Services to Families and Children

Once upon a time there lived a man and woman named James and Martha Brown. They had been married for a long time and were very happy together. Only one thing was missing in their lives. They had no babies of their own, and they had always wanted children to share their home.

One day James and Martha said to each other, "Let's adopt a baby to bring up as our very own."

So they called the adoption agency, a place where there are people who help parents to adopt babies and babies to adopt parents. Mrs. Karen White answered the phone. Martha said to her, "James and I want so much to find a baby who would like to have a mother and father. Will you help us find one?"

Mrs. White said, "Come to my office, and let's talk it over."

So the Browns went to see Mrs. White and told her how much they wanted to adopt a baby. Mrs. White asked them whether they wanted a baby boy or a baby girl. They answered, "It really doesn't matter. We think we would like our first child to be a boy, but if you find a baby girl for us, we will be just as happy."

Mrs. White asked the Browns many questions, and then said, "Many, many people want to adopt children. It will not be easy to find the right baby for you. You may have to wait a while."

A few days later Mrs. White came to visit the Browns at home. She asked them more questions and looked at all the rooms. She seemed especially interested to know where the baby would sleep and play. She liked the kind of home the Browns had.

Several months went by, and the Browns did not hear from Mrs. White. They often said to each other, "I wonder when our baby will be coming."

And Martha Brown would call up Mrs. White and say, "We are still waiting for our baby. Please don't forget about us."

Mrs. White would say, "Please be patient. Your baby will come some day."

Then one day Mrs. White visited the Browns again. They had a good time together. The Browns kept saying to each other, "Surely this means our baby is coming soon." They told Mrs. White that if their baby turned out to be a boy, they would name him Peter, and if it was a girl, her name would be Mary.

Soon after that Mrs. White called the Browns and said, "I have good news for you!

We have a baby boy for you to see. Can you come to my office tomorrow?"

The very next morning, the Browns hurried to Mrs. White's office. First Mrs. White told them all about the baby boy they were going to see. Then she said, "Now go into the next room and see the baby. If you find that he is not *just the right baby for you*, tell me, and we will try to find another."

In the next room the Browns found a rosy, fat baby boy asleep in a crib. He opened his big brown eyes and smiled. Martha Brown picked him up and sat him on her lap. The baby and Martha looked at each other for a long time. James Brown took the baby in his arms, and the baby and James looked at each other for a long time. Then the Browns looked at each other and said, "We don't need to look any further. This is the baby we want."

They went back to Mrs. White's office and said, "We will have everything ready for him by tomorrow and will take him home then."

Karen White was happy.

James and Martha Brown were happy.

The baby was laughing and kicking his legs and wiggling his toes. He looked happy too.

When the Browns left Mrs. White's office, they went right out to a store and bought a carriage and bottles and all the clothes and things that babies need. It was hard for them to wait for the next day to come, but they kept busy fixing up the baby's room so that it was just right.

Bright and early the next morning the Browns went to fetch their baby. They brought him home and fed him milk, cereal, and orange juice, and put him in his crib. Then James and Martha Brown stood there a long time, smiling down at him. Soon he was fast asleep.

They named him Peter. After a few days Peter's new grandfathers and grandmothers, uncles and aunts and cousins came to see him. They all agreed that he was a lovely baby. His parents thought so too.

James and Martha and Peter Brown had wonderful times together. They laughed and played and were very happy indeed. Peter grew so fast and so well that soon he began to crawl, and to walk, and to climb, and to talk.

He loved to play hide-and-seek, hiding behind doors and under beds where no one could find him. But he could always find his daddy.

Every week he would visit his grandfather and grandmother who lived nearby. They always gave him cookies and milk, and said, "Peter Brown, you are a fine young man."

When summer came, Peter went on a long trip to the seaside and paid a visit to his other grandfather and grandmother. He played in the sand with his pail and shovel. The waves and Peter chased each other up and down the beach and kept laughing at each other. These grandparents also thought Peter a fine boy, and they liked to watch him as he splashed in the ocean.

One day James and Martha and Peter were out taking a walk, when a little girl came running by with a kite. Peter wanted to run and play with her. She was a pretty little girl with red hair and freckles.

That night when Peter was in bed asleep, James and Martha said to each other, "Peter liked that little girl we saw today. We should adopt a baby sister, and then she and Peter can play together."

So the next day they called up Mrs. White and said, "We want to find a baby sister for Peter."

And Mrs. White said, "We will gladly try to find a sister for Peter."

Peter was so excited about getting a baby sister that he could hardly wait for the day when she would come. He was now big enough to sleep in a real bed, and he told his mother he would give his crib to his sister.

Almost a year went by, and the Browns were becoming impatient. Mrs. White kept telling them, "I hope you won't have to wait much longer, but more and more people want to adopt babies."

At last Mrs. White called one day and said, "I have a baby girl here who, I think, will be a good sister for Peter. Can you come to see her tomorrow?"

James and Martha Brown went to Mrs. White's office the next day and found waiting for them a bouncing baby girl with soft brown eyes and a happy smile. Right away they said, "We love this baby already." The baby grabbed hold of one of Mr. Brown's fingers and held it tight in her fist. The Browns told Mrs. White they would be back the next day with Peter. They wanted him to see her too.

When Peter saw the baby, he thought she was the best baby he had ever seen. He wanted her for his sister, so he and his mother and father took the baby home.

When Peter woke up the next day, he ran to the crib where his sister was sleeping. Then he ran to his mother and father shouting, "Mommy, Daddy, come and see Peter's baby!"

The Browns remembered that long ago they had decided that the name of their little girl would be Mary. They talked it over with Peter, and he said it was a fine name, so they called the baby Mary.

The Browns gave a big party with ice cream and cake and lots of candy, and grandfathers and grandmothers and cousins and aunts and uncles came. They all thought Mary was a wonderful baby. And Peter showed everybody that now he could almost stand on his head.

Peter had to learn many things about babies. He shared his room and his toys with his sister. And now that he was a big boy and could ride a bike, he let Mary have his old stroller.

Mary grew fast and is now a lively little girl who runs about and plays games. Peter and Mary like to hear the story of how they were adopted. James and Martha and Peter and Mary Brown are a very happy family.